g A GOLDEN BOOK • NEW YORK

rhcbooks.com

ISBN 978-0-7364-4034-9

Printed in the United States of America

10 9 8 7 6 5 4 3 2 1

DISNEY
FROZEN II

Adapted by
Bill Scollon

Illustrated by the
Disney Storybook Art Team

King Agnarr of Arendelle loved telling his daughters, Elsa and Anna, stories of long ago. One night he told them about the *Northuldra*, a people who lived in harmony with the spirits of nature. The story left Anna and Elsa with *many questions*. But it was late, so their mother, Queen Iduna, lulled them to sleep with a lullaby. She sang of a river called Ahtohallan, which held all the answers to the past. Elsa wondered if Ahtohallan knew why she had magical power. "Someone should really try to find it," she said before dozing off.

Many years and adventures later, Arendelle was flourishing.
Elsa was the new ruler, and she and Anna surrounded
themselves with a friendly group—composed of a snowman,
a reindeer, and a mountain man—they called *family*.
One evening, they were all playing *charades*.
Olaf and Kristoff made a great team.

"Teapot!"
"Unicorn!"

Kristoff guessed correctly every time
Olaf rearranged himself into a new shape.

It was Elsa and Anna's turn. As Elsa
stood before the group, she heard a
haunting melody sung by a voice that no
one else seemed to hear. It took her focus
off the game.

When the round was over, Elsa abruptly
excused herself, saying she was tired.

Anna knew her sister wasn't just tired. She opened the door to Elsa's room and saw that she had wrapped herself in their mother's *scarf*.

"You do that when something's wrong," said Anna. "What is it?"

Elsa wanted to tell Anna about the voice but decided against it. Instead, she said she was worried about messing things up.

"You're doing great," Anna assured her.

Elsa smiled. "What would I do without you?" she asked.

"You'll always have me," replied Anna.

Later that night, the voice woke Elsa, louder and more insistent than before. She followed it to the fjord. She needed to know more about it.

Elsa began to sing along with the voice's call. As she did, she felt her magic getting **stronger**. The voice encouraged her to use her power in **new ways**.

Elsa found she could pull moisture out of the air and create wonderful fleeting images made of snow. *How can this be happening?* she thought.

Then Elsa felt the voice pull away
from her. She reached for it and a shock
wave of magic blasted from her in every
direction. The moisture in the air froze
into *crystals* that dotted the sky as far
as she could see. Suddenly, an explosion
of light came from the north.

The **shock wave** woke Anna. When she saw that Elsa was not in her bedroom, she raced for the castle doors. Just as she stumbled into the courtyard, the frozen crystals fell from the sky.

The sound of crashing ice crystals brought the villagers out of their homes as well. All around them, lanterns suddenly flickered out, and the water in the fountains began to dry up.

The sisters found each other, and it was clear to them that something was very wrong. The ground shook and the wind blew the villagers, pushing everyone toward the cliffs.

After they were all safe, Elsa told her sister about the voice.

"A voice?" asked Anna. "What kind of voice? What did it say?"

Elsa revealed that the voice hadn't said anything—it had
simply shown her the Enchanted Forest. She knew she needed
to travel there.

"Not without us, you don't," Anna said.

The ground rumbled again, but this time it was the
mountain trolls rolling through the pass. *Grand Pabbie*
went straight to Elsa.

"Much about the past is not what it seems," Pabbie said. "When one can see no future, all one can do is the next right thing."

Elsa had to find the voice. "And this time, Anna, I am not afraid," she said.

Grand Pabbie told Anna he would take care of the villagers but she needed to watch over Elsa.

"I won't let anything happen to her," Anna promised.

At dawn, Elsa, Anna, Olaf, Kristoff, and Sven left
Arendelle, headed due north. They traveled *day and night*.
Their mission was too important—the stakes too high—
to stop for rest.

Olaf tried to *lighten the mood*. "Who's into trivia?"
he asked, but he didn't wait for a response. "I am! Okay!"

The snowman kept up a never-ending chatter, revealing *fun facts* he had discovered since learning to read. "Did you know that water has memory?" Olaf said. "Did you know men are six times more likely to be struck by lightning? Sorry, Kristoff!"

As they went over a small hill, Elsa heard the voice again. She asked Kristoff to stop the wagon. Straight ahead, the sun revealed the *Enchanted Forest*, shrouded in a heavy mist.

Elsa raced across the plain with Anna right behind her, but they stopped before reaching the mist. "We do this together, okay?" Anna said.

"Together," Elsa replied.

At once, the mist began to part.

Kristoff, Olaf, and Sven hurried to join Anna and Elsa. The group stared as four *giant stone columns* were revealed.

The friends moved slowly toward the monoliths. But once they were inside the mist, it closed around them. They were trapped!

They didn't have time to be concerned, as the mist began to push the friends into the unknown!

They eventually stumbled into a wooded area.
Everyone looked around in amazement. They had
entered the Enchanted Forest!

Suddenly, the snowman was swept up by a gust of air.
"Olaf!" Elsa cried, rushing toward him.

It was the *Wind Spirit*! Moments later, the whole
group was caught in its vortex.

Elsa sent a blast of magic that pushed everyone out of the whirlwind—except her. She filled the vortex with a steady stream of snow and slowed its spinning. Then she threw her arms open and snow flew everywhere.

Elsa was free. And she was surrounded by ice sculptures depicting beautiful moments frozen in time.

"What's that thing you say, Olaf?" Anna asked.

"Water has memory," he said.

As Anna and Elsa walked among the sculptures, one in particular caught their attention. It showed their father as a teenager. He was being rescued by a girl who wore a scarf that was just like their mother's.

They suddenly heard a loud banging. Reindeer quickly *surrounded* Elsa and the others as people emerged from the bushes. They were the Northuldra! Anna grabbed an ice sword from one of the sculptures.

"Lower your weapon," said a Northuldra woman named Honeymaren.

Seconds later, soldiers from Arendelle, in faded and tattered uniforms, appeared.

"And you lower yours," Lieutenant Mattias of the Arendellians said to Honeymaren.

But another Northuldra, Yelana, sneaked up behind them.

"Threatening my people again, Lieutenant?" she said.

The two groups charged, both wanting to be the first to capture the sisters and their friends. Elsa used her magic to make the ground slick, causing the Northuldra and the Arendellian soldiers to slip and fall.

"That was magic!" Mattias cried.

As Mattias got to his feet, Anna asked, "Do I know you?"
She and Elsa walked over to him.

Then it hit her. His portrait was in the castle. "You were
our father's *official guard*!" Anna exclaimed.

"I see him. I see him in your faces," Mattias said.

The young Northuldra were also eager to meet Anna and Elsa. Honeymaren approached them and asked about the scarf Anna was carrying. Anna explained that it had been given to her father, who had then given it to her mother.

It was remarkable to all that a traditional Northuldra scarf was cherished by an Arendellian queen. Maybe the two sides were *more alike than different*.

Without warning, a bright light shot out from behind a tree. It was the Fire Spirit! Everything it touched burst into flame. People scattered, but Elsa stayed to *battle the blaze* with her magic.

The Northuldra reindeer panicked and ran. Kristoff jumped onto Sven and took off after them.

Elsa spotted the tiny Fire Spirit, a *salamander*, under a rocky overhang.

Elsa held out her hand and the spirit cautiously climbed onto it. She smiled and sprinkled the salamander with snowflakes.

All of a sudden, Elsa heard the voice . . . and so did the Fire Spirit! The two of them turned toward its calling.

"We have to go north," Elsa said. It was time to move on.

Elsa started walking. Even though Kristoff and Sven were away from the camp, Anna and Olaf knew they had to leave immediately with Elsa.

It felt as if they had been walking for hours when a distressing sight came into view—the *wreckage* of an Arendellian ship. When they got closer, Elsa and Anna realized it was their parents' ship! Inside, Anna found a map. Ahtohallan, the river from their mother's lullaby, was clearly marked on it.

Elsa was devastated. "This was my fault. They were looking for answers about *me*!"

"Hey, you are not responsible for their choices," said Anna.

Elsa let that sink in. She knew Anna was right. But she also knew that the next part of the journey would be the most dangerous. She had to go *alone*. If anything happened to Anna, she wouldn't be able to bear it.

She conjured up an ice boat beneath Anna and Olaf and sent them down a dry riverbed.

Anna reached for something, anything, to stop their boat. But they slipped into a quickly flowing river that took them farther from Elsa.

As their ice boat continued downstream, Anna spotted *Earth Giants* sleeping along the shore. The giants stirred as Anna and Olaf drifted silently by. As perilous as the moment was, Anna couldn't help wondering what dangers Elsa was facing.

Elsa had, in fact, reached the Dark Sea. Its *ferocious* waves made it nearly impossible for her to cross. Elsa was determined, but time and time again the sea pushed her back, and then it pulled her under!

She managed to reach the surface and create an ice slide, but when the waves broke it, she dove straight into the water, not noticing an enormous creature watching her.

Below the waves, Elsa was confronted by a looming spirit that took the form of a horse—the *Water Nokk*!

The spirit charged at Elsa over and over, but Elsa didn't surrender. She summoned all her power to create an ice bridle, which she hooked onto the massive horse.

At last, the Water Nokk responded to Elsa's commands. *Together*, they galloped to the other side of the Dark Sea.

Elsa had reached Ahtohallan—and the voice that had been calling to her. The answers to all her questions were there, just as her mother's lullaby had promised. But more than the truth about her magic, *Elsa also discovered peace*—a peace she couldn't wait to share with her sister, the spirits, and spread throughout the kingdom.

Meanwhile, Anna and Olaf had found refuge in a cave. A
twinkle of snowflakes rushed in and formed an *ice sculpture*.
It was a signal from Elsa that she was safe, and soon they would
all be together again.